Alfie

Mr Hoppy

Pet-shop Owner

Mrs Silver

The Tortoise-catcher

ROALD DAHL

Esio Trot

Illustrated by Quentin Blake

PUFFIN BOOKS

Find out more about Roald Dahl
by visiting the web site at
www.roalddahl.com

PUFFIN BOOKS

Published by the Penguin Group
Penguin Books Ltd, 80 Strand, London WC2R 0RL, England
Penguin Putnam Inc., 375 Hudson Street, New York, New York 10014, USA
Penguin Books Australia Ltd, 250 Camberwell Road, Camberwell, Victoria 3124, Australia
Penguin Books Canada Ltd, 10 Alcorn Avenue, Toronto, Ontario, Canada M4V 3B2
Penguin Books India (P) Ltd, 11 Community Centre, Panchsheel Park, New Delhi – 110 017, India
Penguin Books (NZ) Ltd, Cnr Rosedale and Airborne Roads, Albany, Auckland, New Zealand
Penguin Books (South Africa) (Pty) Ltd, 24 Sturdee Avenue, Rosebank 2196, South Africa

Penguin Books Ltd, Registered Offices: 80 Strand, London WC2R 0RL, England

www.penguin.com

First published by Jonathan Cape Ltd 1990
Published in Puffin Books 1991
This edition published 2001
34

Text copyright © Roald Dahl Nominee Ltd, 1990
Illustrations copyright © Quentin Blake, 1990
All rights reserved

Set in Monotype Baskerville

The moral right of the author and illustrator has been asserted

Made and printed in England by Clays Ltd, St Ives plc

British Library Cataloguing in Publication Data
A CIP catalogue record for this book is available from the British Library

ISBN 0–141–31133–9

To Clover and Luke

Author's Note

Some years ago, when my own children were small, we usually kept a tortoise or two in the garden. In those days, a pet tortoise was a common sight crawling about on the family lawn or in the back yard. You could buy them quite cheaply in any pet-shop and they were probably the least troublesome of all childhood pets, and quite harmless.

Tortoises used to be brought into England by the thousand, packed in crates, and they came mostly from North Africa. But not many years ago a law was passed that made it illegal to bring any tortoises into the country. This was not done to protect us. The little tortoise was not a danger to anybody. It was done purely out of kindness to the tortoise itself. You see, the traders who brought them in used to cram hundreds of them tightly into the packing-crates without food or water and in such horrible conditions that a great many of them always died on the sea-journey over. So rather than allow this cruelty to go on, the Government stopped the whole business.

The things you are going to read about in this story all happened in the days when anyone could go out and buy a nice little tortoise from a pet-shop.

ESIO TROT

Mr Hoppy lived in a small flat high up in a tall concrete building. He lived alone. He had always been a lonely man and now that he was retired from work he was more lonely than ever.

There were two loves in Mr Hoppy's life. One was the flowers he grew on his balcony. They grew in pots and tubs and baskets, and in summer the little balcony became a riot of colour.

Mr Hoppy's second love was a secret he kept entirely to himself.

The balcony immediately below Mr Hoppy's jutted out a good bit further from the building than his own, so Mr Hoppy always had a fine view of what was going on down there. This balcony belonged to an attractive middle-aged lady called Mrs Silver. Mrs Silver was a widow who also lived alone. And although she didn't know it, it was she who was the object of Mr Hoppy's secret love. He had loved her from his balcony for many years, but he was a very shy man and he had never been able to bring himself to give her even the smallest hint of his love.

Every morning, Mr Hoppy and Mrs Silver exchanged polite conversation, the one looking down from above, the other looking up, but that was as far as it ever went. The distance between their balconies might not have been more than a few yards, but to Mr Hoppy it seemed like a million miles. He longed to invite Mrs Silver up for a cup of tea and a biscuit, but every time he was about to form the words on his lips, his courage failed him. As I said, he was a very very shy man.

Oh, if only, he kept telling himself, if only he could do something tremendous like saving her life or rescuing her from a gang of armed thugs, if only he could perform some great feat that would make him a hero in her eyes. If only . . .

The trouble with Mrs Silver was that she gave all her love to somebody else, and that somebody was a small tortoise called Alfie. Every day, when Mr Hoppy looked over his balcony and saw Mrs Silver whispering endearments to Alfie and stroking his shell, he felt absurdly jealous. He wouldn't even have minded becoming a tortoise himself if it meant Mrs Silver stroking his shell each morning and whispering endearments to him.

Alfie had been with Mrs Silver for years and he lived on her balcony summer and winter. Planks had been placed around the sides of the balcony so that Alfie could walk about without toppling over the edge, and in one corner there was a little house into which Alfie would crawl every night to keep warm.

When the colder weather came along in November, Mrs Silver would fill Alfie's house with dry hay, and the tortoise would crawl in there and bury himself deep under the hay and go to sleep for months on end

without food or water. This is called hibernating.

In early spring, when Alfie felt the warmer weather through his shell, he would wake up and crawl very slowly out of his house on to the balcony. And Mrs Silver would clap her hands with joy and cry out, 'Welcome back, my darling one! Oh, how I have missed you!'

It was at times like these that Mr Hoppy wished more than ever that he could change places with Alfie and become a tortoise.

Now we come to a certain bright morning in May when something happened that changed and indeed electrified Mr Hoppy's life. He was leaning over his balcony-rail watching Mrs Silver serving Alfie his breakfast.

'Here's the heart of the lettuce for you, my lovely,' she was saying. 'And here's a slice of fresh tomato and a piece of crispy celery.'

'Good morning, Mrs Silver,' Mr Hoppy said. 'Alfie's looking well this morning.'

'Isn't he gorgeous!' Mrs Silver said, looking up and beaming at him.

'Absolutely gorgeous,' Mr Hoppy said, not meaning it. And now, as he looked down at Mrs Silver's smiling face gazing up into his own, he thought for the thousandth time how pretty she was, how sweet and gentle and full of kindness, and his heart ached with love.

'I do so wish he would *grow* a little faster,' Mrs Silver was saying. 'Every spring, when he wakes up from his winter sleep, I weigh him on the kitchen scales. And do you know that in all the eleven years I've had him he's not gained more than *three ounces*! That's almost *nothing*!'

'What does he weigh now?' Mr Hoppy asked her.

'Just thirteen ounces,' Mrs Silver answered. 'About as much as a grapefruit.'

'Yes, well, tortoises are very slow growers,' Mr Hoppy said solemnly. 'But they can live for a hundred years.'

'I know that,' Mrs Silver said. 'But I do so wish he would grow just a little bit bigger. He's such a tiny wee fellow.'

'He seems just fine as he is,' Mr Hoppy said.

'No, he's *not* just fine!' Mrs Silver cried. 'Try to

think how miserable it must make him feel to be so titchy! Everyone wants to grow up.'

'You really *would* love him to grow bigger, wouldn't you?' Mr Hoppy said, and even as he said it his mind suddenly went *click* and an amazing idea came rushing into his head.

'Of course I would!' Mrs Silver cried. 'I'd give *anything* to make it happen! Why, I've seen pictures of giant tortoises that are so huge people can ride on their backs! If Alfie were to see those he'd turn green with envy!'

Mr Hoppy's mind was spinning like a fly-wheel. Here, surely, was his big chance! Grab it, he told himself. Grab it quick!

'Mrs Silver,' he said. 'I do actually happen to know how to make tortoises grow faster, if that's really what you want.'

'You do?' she cried. 'Oh, please tell me! Am I feeding him the wrong things?'

'I worked in North Africa once,' Mr Hoppy said. 'That's where all these tortoises in England come from, and a bedouin tribesman told me the secret.'

'Tell me!' cried Mrs Silver. 'I beg you to tell me, Mr Hoppy! I'll be your slave for life.'

When he heard the words *your slave for life*, a little shiver of excitement swept through Mr Hoppy. 'Wait there,' he said. 'I'll have to go in and write something down for you.'

In a couple of minutes Mr Hoppy was back on the balcony with a sheet of paper in his hand. 'I'm going to lower it to you on a bit of string,' he said, 'or it might blow away. Here it comes.'

Mrs Silver caught the paper and held it up in front of her. This is what she read:

ESIO TROT, ESIO TROT,
TEG REGGIB REGGIB!
EMOC NO, ESIO TROT,
WORG PU, FFUP PU, TOOHS PU!
GNIRPS PU, WOLB PU, LLEWS PU!
EGROG! ELZZUG! FFUTS! PLUG!
TUP NO TAF, ESIO TROT, TUP NO TAF!
TEG NO, TEG NO! ELBBOG DOOF!

'What *does* it mean?' she asked. 'Is it another language?'

'It's tortoise language,' Mr Hoppy said.

'Tortoises are very backward creatures. Therefore they can only understand words that are written backwards. That's obvious, isn't it?'

'I suppose so,' Mrs Silver said, bewildered.

'Esio trot is simply tortoise spelled backwards,' Mr Hoppy said. 'Look at it.'

'So it is,' Mrs Silver said.

'The other words are spelled backwards, too,' Mr Hoppy said. 'If you turn them round into human language, they simply say:

TORTOISE, TORTOISE,
GET BIGGER BIGGER!
COME ON, TORTOISE,
GROW UP, PUFF UP, SHOOT UP!
SPRING UP, BLOW UP, SWELL UP!
GORGE! GUZZLE! STUFF! GULP!
PUT ON FAT, TORTOISE, PUT ON FAT!
GET ON, GET ON! GOBBLE FOOD!'

Mrs Silver examined the magic words on the paper more closely. 'I guess you're right,' she said. 'How clever. But there's an awful lot of poos in it. Are they something special?'

'Poo is a very strong word in any language,' Mr Hoppy said, 'especially with tortoises. Now what you have to do, Mrs Silver, is hold Alfie up to your face and whisper these words to him three times a day, morning, noon and night. Let me hear you practise them.'

Very slowly and stumbling a little over the strange words, Mrs Silver read the whole message out loud in tortoise language.

'Not bad,' Mr Hoppy said. 'But try to get a little more expression into it when you say it to Alfie. If you do it properly I'll bet you anything you like that in a few months' time he'll be twice as big as he is now.'

'I'll try it,' Mrs Silver said. 'I'll try anything. Of course I will. But I can't believe it'll work.'

'You wait and see,' Mr Hoppy said, smiling at her.

Back in his flat, Mr Hoppy was simply quivering all over with excitement. *Your slave for life*, he kept repeating to himself. What bliss!

But there was a lot of work to be done before that happened.

The only furniture in Mr Hoppy's small living-room was a table and two chairs. These he moved into his bedroom. Then he went out and bought a sheet of thick canvas and spread it over the entire living-room floor to protect his carpet.

Next, he got out the telephone-book and wrote down the address of every pet-shop in the city. There were fourteen of them altogether.

It took him two days to visit each pet-shop and choose his tortoises. He wanted a great many, at least one hundred, perhaps more. And he had to choose them very carefully.

To you and me there is not much difference between one tortoise and another. They differ only in their size and in the colour of their shells. Alfie had a darkish shell, so Mr Hoppy chose only the darker-shelled tortoises for his great collection.

Size, of course, was everything. Mr Hoppy chose all sorts of different sizes, some weighing only slightly more than Alfie's thirteen ounces, others a great deal more, but he didn't want any that weighed less.

'Feed them cabbage leaves,' the pet-shop owners told him. 'That's all they'll need. And a bowl of water.'

When he had finished, Mr Hoppy, in his enthusiasm, had bought no less than one hundred and forty tortoises and he carried them home in baskets, ten or fifteen at a time. He had to make a lot of trips and he was quite exhausted at the end of it all, but it was worth it. Boy, was it worth it! And what an amazing sight his living-room was when they were all in there together! The floor was swarming with tortoises of different sizes,

some walking slowly about and exploring, some munching cabbage leaves, others drinking water from a big shallow dish. They made just the faintest rustling sound as they moved over the canvas sheet, but that was all. Mr Hoppy had to pick his way carefully on his toes between this moving sea of brown shells whenever he walked across the room. But enough of that. He must get on with the job.

Before he retired Mr Hoppy had been a mechanic in a bus-garage. And now he went back to his old place of work and asked his mates if he might use his old bench for an hour or two.

What he had to do now was to make something that would reach down from his own balcony to Mrs Silver's balcony and pick up a tortoise. This was not difficult for a mechanic like Mr Hoppy.

First he made two metal claws or fingers, and these he attached to the end of a long metal tube. He ran two stiff wires down inside the tube and connected them to the metal claws in such a way that when you pulled the wires, the claws closed, and when you pushed them, the claws opened. The wires were joined to a handle at the other end of the tube. It was all very simple.

Mr Hoppy was ready to begin.

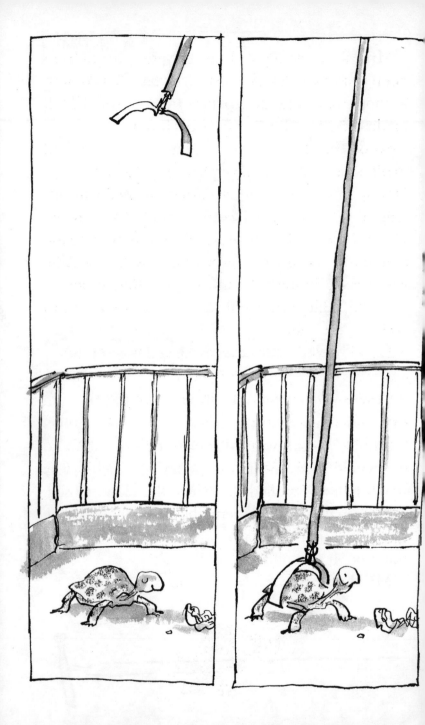

Mrs Silver had a part-time job. She worked from noon until five o'clock every weekday afternoon in a shop that sold newspapers and sweets. That made things a lot easier for Mr Hoppy.

So on that first exciting afternoon, after he had made sure that Mrs Silver had gone to work, Mr Hoppy went out on to his balcony armed with his long metal pole. He called this his tortoise-catcher. He leaned over the balcony railings and lowered the pole down on to Mrs Silver's balcony below. Alfie was basking in the pale sunlight over to one side.

'Hello, Alfie,' Mr Hoppy said. 'You are about to go for a little ride.'

He wiggled the tortoise-catcher till it was right above Alfie. He pushed the hand-lever so that the claws opened wide. Then he lowered the two claws neatly over Alfie's shell and pulled the lever. The claws closed tightly over the shell like two fingers of a hand. He hauled Alfie up on to his own balcony. It was easy.

Mr Hoppy weighed Alfie on his own kitchen scales just to make sure that Mrs Silver's figure of thirteen ounces was correct. It was.

Now, holding Alfie in one hand, he picked his way carefully through his huge collection of tortoises to find one that first of all had the same colour shell as Alfie's and secondly weighed *exactly two ounces more*.

Two ounces is not much. It is less than a smallish hen's egg weighs. But, you see, the important thing in Mr Hoppy's plan was to make sure that the new tortoise was bigger than Alfie but only a *tiny bit* bigger. The difference had to be so small that Mrs Silver wouldn't notice it.

From his vast collection, it was not difficult for Mr Hoppy to find just the tortoise he wanted. He wanted one that weighed fifteen ounces exactly on his kitchen scales, no more and no less. When he had got it, he put it on the kitchen table beside Alfie, and even he could hardly tell that one was bigger than the other. But it *was* bigger. It was bigger by two ounces. This was Tortoise Number 2.

Mr Hoppy took Tortoise Number 2 out on to the balcony and gripped it in the claws of his tortoise-catcher. Then he lowered it on to Mrs Silver's balcony, right beside a nice fresh lettuce.

Tortoise Number 2 had never eaten tender juicy lettuce leaves before. It had only had thick old cabbage leaves. It loved the lettuce and started chomping away at it with great gusto.

There followed a rather nervous two hours' wait for Mrs Silver to return from work.

Would she see any difference between the new tortoise and Alfie? It was going to be a tense moment.

Out on to her balcony swept Mrs Silver.

'Alfie, my darling!' she cried out. 'Mummy's back! Have you missed me?'

Mr Hoppy, peering over his railing, but well hidden between two huge potted plants, held his breath.

The new tortoise was still chomping away at the lettuce.

'My my, Alfie, you do seem hungry today,' Mrs Silver was saying. 'It must be Mr Hoppy's magic words I've been whispering to you.'

Mr Hoppy watched as Mrs Silver picked the tortoise up and stroked his shell. Then she fished Mr Hoppy's piece of paper out of her pocket, and holding the tortoise very close to her face, she whispered, reading from the paper:

'ESIO TROT, ESIO TROT,
TEG REGGIB REGGIB!
EMOC NO, ESIO TROT,
WORG PU, FFUP PU, TOOHS PU!
GNIRPS PU, WOLB PU, LLEWS PU!
EGROG! ELZZUG! FFUTS! PLUG!
TUP NO TAF, ESIO TROT, TUP NO TAF!
TEG NO, TEG NO! ELBBOG DOOF!'

Mr Hoppy
popped his head
out of the foliage
and called out,
'Good evening,
Mrs Silver. How
is Alfie tonight?'

'Oh, he's lovely,' Mrs Silver said, looking up and beaming. 'And he's developing *such* an appetite! I've never seen him eat like this before! It must be the magic words.'

'You never know,' Mr Hoppy said darkly. 'You never know.'

Mr Hoppy waited seven whole days before he made his next move.

On the afternoon of the seventh day, when Mrs Silver was at work, he lifted Tortoise Number 2 from the balcony below and brought it into his living-room. Number 2 had weighed exactly *fifteen* ounces. He must now find one that weighed exactly *seventeen* ounces, two ounces more.

From his enormous collection, he easily found a seventeen-ounce tortoise and once again he made sure the shells matched in colour. Then he lowered Tortoise Number 3 on to Mrs Silver's balcony.

As you will have guessed by now, Mr Hoppy's secret was a very simple one. If a creature grows slowly enough – I mean very very slowly indeed – then you'll never notice that it has grown at all, especially if you see it every day.

It's the same with children. They are actually growing taller every week, but their mothers never notice it until they grow out of their clothes.

Slowly does it, Mr Hoppy told himself. Don't hurry it.

So this is how things went over the next eight weeks.

In the beginning

ALFIE   weight 13 ounces

End of first week

TORTOISE NO. 2   weight 15 ounces

End of second week

TORTOISE NO. 3   weight 17 ounces

End of third week

TORTOISE NO. 4   weight 19 ounces

End of fourth week

TORTOISE NO. 5   weight 21 ounces

End of fifth week

TORTOISE NO. 6   weight 23 ounces

TORTOISE NO. 7   weight 25 ounces

End of seventh week

TORTOISE NO. 8   weight 27 ounces

Alfie's weight was thirteen ounces. Tortoise Number 8 was twenty-seven ounces. Very slowly, over seven weeks, Mrs Silver's pet had more than doubled in size and the good lady hadn't noticed a thing.

Even to Mr Hoppy, peering down over his railing, Tortoise Number 8 looked pretty big. It was amazing that Mrs Silver had hardly noticed anything at all during the great operation. Only once had she looked up and said, 'You know, Mr Hoppy, I do believe he's getting a bit bigger. What do you think?'

'I can't see a lot of difference myself,' Mr Hoppy had answered casually.

But now perhaps it was time to call a halt, and that evening Mr Hoppy was just about to go out and suggest to Mrs Silver that she ought to weigh Alfie when a startled cry from the balcony below brought him outside fast.

'Look!' Mrs Silver was shouting. 'Alfie's too big to get through the door of his little house! He must have grown enormously!'

'Weigh him,' Mr Hoppy ordered. 'Take him in and weigh him quick.'

Mrs Silver did just that, and in half a minute she was back holding the tortoise in both hands and waving it above her head and shouting, 'Guess what, Mr Hoppy! Guess what! He weighs twenty-seven ounces! He's twice as big as he was before! Oh, you darling!' she cried, stroking the tortoise. 'Oh, you great big wonderful boy! Just look what clever Mr Hoppy has done for you!'

Mr Hoppy suddenly felt very brave. 'Mrs Silver,' he said. 'Do you think I could pop down to your balcony and hold Alfie myself?'

'Why, of course you can!' Mrs Silver cried. 'Come down at once.'

Mr Hoppy rushed down the stairs and Mrs Silver opened the door to him. Together they went out on to the balcony. 'Just look at him!' Mrs Silver said proudly. 'Isn't he grand!'

'He's a big good-sized tortoise now,' Mr Hoppy said.

'And *you* did it!' Mrs Silver cried. 'You're a miracle-man, you are indeed!'

'But what *am* I going to do about his house?' Mrs Silver said. 'He must have a house to go into at night, but now he can't get through the door.'

They were standing on the balcony looking at the tortoise, who was trying to push his way into his house. But he was too big.

'I shall have to enlarge the door,' Mrs Silver said.

'Don't do that,' Mr Hoppy said. 'You mustn't go chopping up such a pretty little house. After all, he only needs to be just a tiny bit smaller and he could get in easily.'

'How can he possibly get smaller?' Mrs Silver asked.

'That's simple,' Mr Hoppy said. 'Change the

magic words. Instead of telling him to get bigger
and bigger, tell him to get a bit smaller. But in
tortoise language of course.'

'Will that work?'

'Of course it'll work.'

'Tell me exactly what I have to say, Mr Hoppy.'

Mr Hoppy got out a piece of paper and a pencil
and wrote:

ESIO TROT, ESIO TROT,
TEG A TIB RELLAMS, A TIB RELLAMS.

'That'll do it, Mrs Silver,' he said, handing her the paper.

'I don't mind trying it,' Mrs Silver said. 'But look here, I wouldn't want him to get titchy small all over again, Mr Hoppy.'

'He won't, dear lady, he won't,' Mr Hoppy said. 'Say it only tonight and tomorrow morning and then see what happens. We might be lucky.'

'If it works,' Mrs Silver said, touching him softly on the arm, 'then you are the cleverest man alive.'

The next afternoon, as soon as Mrs Silver had gone to work, Mr Hoppy lifted the tortoise up from her balcony and carried it inside. All he had to do now was to find one that was a shade smaller, so that it would just go through the door of the little house.

He chose one and lowered it down with his tortoise-catcher. Then, still gripping the tortoise, he tested it to see if it would go through the door. It wouldn't.

He chose another. Again he tested it. This one went through nicely. Good. He placed the tortoise in the middle of the balcony beside a nice piece of lettuce and went inside to await Mrs Silver's home-coming.

That evening, Mr Hoppy was watering his plants on the balcony when suddenly he heard Mrs Silver's shouts from below, shrill with excitement.

'Mr Hoppy! Mr Hoppy! Where are you?' she was shouting. 'Just look at this!'

Mr Hoppy popped his head over the railing and said, 'What's up?'

'Oh, Mr Hoppy, it's worked!' she was crying. 'Your magic words have worked again on Alfie! He can now get through the door of his little house! It's a miracle!'

'Can I come down and look?' Mr Hoppy shouted back.

'Come down at once, my dear man!' Mrs Silver answered. 'Come down and see the wonders you have worked upon my darling Alfie!'

Mr
Hoppy
turned and
ran from the
balcony into the
living-room, jumping
on tip-toe like a ballet-
dancer between the sea of
tortoises that covered the floor. He
flung open his front door and flew down
the stairs two at a time with the love-songs of
a thousand cupids ringing in his ears. *This is it!*
he whispered to himself under his breath. *The greatest
moment of my life is coming up now! I mustn't bish it. I
mustn't bosh it! I must keep very calm!* When he was
three-quarters way down the stairs he caught sight
of Mrs Silver already standing at the open door
waiting to welcome him with a huge smile on her
face. She flung her arms around him and cried out,
'You really are the most wonderful man I've ever
met! You can do anything! Come in at once and let
me make you a cup of tea. That's the very least you
deserve!'

Seated in a comfortable armchair in Mrs Silver's
parlour, sipping his tea, Mr Hoppy was all of a twit-
ter. He looked at the lovely lady sitting opposite him
and smiled at her. She smiled right back at him.

That smile of hers, so warm and friendly, suddenly gave him the courage he needed, and he said, 'Mrs Silver, please will you marry me?'

'Why, Mr Hoppy!' she cried. 'I didn't think you'd ever get round to asking me! Of course I'll marry you!'

Mr Hoppy got rid of his teacup and the two of them stood up and embraced warmly in the middle of the room.

'It's all due to Alfie,' Mrs Silver said, slightly breathless.

'Good old Alfie,' Mr Hoppy said. 'We'll keep him for ever.'

The next afternoon, Mr Hoppy took all his other tortoises back to the pet-shops and said they could have them for nothing. Then he cleaned up his living-room, leaving not a leaf of cabbage nor a trace of tortoise.

A few weeks later, Mrs Silver became Mrs Hoppy and the two of them lived very happily ever after.

P.S. I expect you are wondering what happened to little Alfie, the first of them all. Well, he was bought a week later from one of the pet-shops by a small girl called Roberta Squibb, and he settled down in Roberta's garden. Every day she fed him lettuce and tomato slices and crispy celery, and in the winters he hibernated in a box of dried leaves in the tool-shed.

That was a long time ago. Roberta has grown up and is now married and has two children of her own. She lives in another house, but Alfie is still with her, still the much-loved family pet, and Roberta reckons that by now he must be about thirty years old. It has taken him all that time to grow to twice the size he was when Mrs Silver had him. But he made it in the end.

ROALD DAHL

BORN: Llandaff, Wales, 1916.
SCHOOLS: Llandaff Cathedral School, St Peter's, Repton.
JOBS: Shell Oil Company representative in East Africa, RAF fighter pilot in Second World War, air attaché, author.

When Roald Dahl's own children were small, they used to keep a pet tortoise or two in the garden. This was long before they made it illegal to bring tortoises into England. As well as a writer, Dahl was a keen inventor and he did actually build the tortoise-catcher in this story – except that he used it for picking things up from the floor, to save bending his aching back!

Roald Dahl died in 1990 at the age of seventy-four.

This was the motto that he lived by:

> My candle burns at both ends
> It will not last the night
> But ah my foes and oh my friends
> It gives a lovely light.

more about **Roald Dahl** by visiting the web site at
www.roalddahl.com